Show-Jumping Dreams

To Beauty, who helped me gain confidence—SB

GROSSET & DUNLAP
Published by the Penguin Group
Penguin Group (USA) Inc., 375 Hudson Street, New York, New York 10014, USA
Penguin Group (Canada), 90 Eglinton Avenue East, Suite 700, Toronto, Ontario M4P 2Y3, Canada
(a division of Pearson Penguin Canada Inc.)
Penguin Books Ltd, 80 Strand, London WC2R 0RL, England
Penguin Ireland, 25 St Stephen's Green, Dublin 2, Ireland (a division of Penguin Books Ltd)
Penguin Group (Australia), 707 Collins Street, Melbourne, Victoria 3008, Australia
(a division of Pearson Australia Group Pty Ltd)
Penguin Books India Pvt Ltd, 11 Community Centre, Panchsheel Park, New Delhi—110 017, India
Penguin Group (NZ), 67 Apollo Drive, Rosedale, Auckland 0632, New Zealand
(a division of Pearson New Zealand Ltd)
Penguin Books (South Africa), Rosebank Office Park, 181 Jan Smuts Avenue,
Parktown North 2193, South Africa
Penguin China, B7 Jiaming Center, 27 East Third Ring Road North,
Chaoyang District, Beijing 100020, China

Penguin Books Ltd, Registered Offices: 80 Strand, London WC2R 0RL, England

Text copyright © 2009 by Sue Bentley. Illustrations copyright © 2009 by Angela Swan. Cover illustration © 2009 by Andrew Farley. First printed in Great Britain in 2009 by Penguin Books Ltd. First published in the United States in 2013 by Grosset & Dunlap, a division of Penguin Young Readers Group, 345 Hudson Street, New York, New York 10014. GROSSET & DUNLAP is a trademark of Penguin Group (USA) Inc. Printed in the U.S.A.

Library of Congress Cataloging-in-Publication Data is available.

ISBN 978-0-448-46208-0   10 9 8 7 6 5 4 3 2

Show-Jumping Dreams

SUE BENTLEY

illustrated by Angela Swan

Grosset & Dunlap
An Imprint of Penguin Group (USA) Inc.

Prologue

Comet folded his gorgeous golden wings as his shining hooves touched down on the grassy plain. The magic pony gave a whinny of excitement. It felt good to be home on Rainbow Mist Island.

But his happiness lasted only a moment as he thought about his twin sister. Destiny had been lost for so long. Surely she must have returned safely by now.

The scent of the sweet grass reminded Comet that he was very hungry, so he lowered his head and began eating. Sunbeams slanted through the swirling multicolored mist that gave the island its name. They gleamed on his cream coat and gold mane and tail.

Chewing, Comet looked up, scanning the landscape for signs of any of the other horses that belonged to the Lightning Herd. His large deep-violet eyes widened as he caught a movement.

Comet could see a shadow stretching across the grass. His coat twitched with nerves as he stiffened. Was it a magic pony or one of the dark horses who wanted to steal the Lightning Herd's magic?

Comet hesitated, weighing the danger. "Destiny?"

The magic pony's lonely heart quickened with longing as he thought of his twin sister who he missed so much. He snorted, deciding to take a risk, and cantered toward the trees.

Just as Comet reached them, the low branches parted and an older horse with a wise expression and calm gold eyes stepped out.

"Blaze!" Swallowing his sadness, Comet bowed his head before the leader of the Lightning Herd.

"I am glad to see you again, my young friend," Blaze said in a deep neigh. "But I am afraid that Destiny has not returned to us."

Comet sighed deeply. "She must still think she is in trouble for losing the stone."

The Stone of Power protected the Lightning Herd from the dark horses. Destiny had accidentally lost it when she and Comet were cloud-racing. Comet recovered the stone, but Destiny had already fled.

Blaze nodded gravely. "I do not think she will come back, unless you find her and explain all is now well."

Comet's beautiful violet eyes flashed with purpose. "I will go to the other world and search for her!"

"We must ask for the stone's help to find where she is hiding." Blaze stamped his foot and pawed at the grass. A fiery opal appeared, which swirled with flashes of multicolored light.

The magic pony looked down and peered deeply into the rainbow. The stone grew larger and rays of dazzling light spread outward.

An image formed in the glowing center. Comet gasped as he saw Destiny standing beneath a tree in a world far away.

"I will leave at once!" he whinnied.

There was a bright flash of dazzling violet light, and rainbow mist surrounded Comet. The pale cream pony, with his flowing golden mane and tail and gleaming gold-feathered wings, disappeared. In his place stood a handsome palomino pony with a warm caramel-colored coat, a sandy mane and tail, and glowing deep-violet eyes.

"Use this disguise. Find your twin sister and return with her safely," Blaze urged.

"I will!" Comet vowed.

The magic pony's caramel coat
bloomed with violet sparks. Comet
snorted as he felt the power building
inside him. And the shimmering rainbow
mist whooshed into a whirlpool as it
drew Comet in . . .

Chapter ONE

"Go on, Alex! Go for it!" Zoe cried. With her best friend shouting encouragement, Alexandra Judd gritted her teeth and concentrated hard as she rode toward the final fence. If Pasha soared over this one, too, it would be a clear round.

Her mom and dad were in the crowd watching the horse show. She hoped she

could make them proud. It would be
great to win a trophy to take home.

Alex sat tall, looked straight ahead,
and kept her heels down. Strands of her
shoulder-length brown hair blew out
from under her riding hat.

"One! Two! Th—" she said under her
breath. "Oh!" At the last moment, her
chestnut pony seemed to miss a step.

Pasha swung her hind legs sideways,
just avoiding banging into the fence. But

with a whinny of pain, the pony sank on to her haunches. Alex only just managed to stay on as Pasha scrambled to her feet and stood with her head hanging down.

Alex gasped with dismay as she realized that something was really wrong.

Dismounting quickly and trying to fight panic, she led her pony away from the course. "Poor girl. Did you hurt yourself?" she said gently. "Come on, take it slow. Let's get the vet to look at you. She'll make you feel better."

As she led the limping pony to one side, her mom and dad were already racing toward her. Alex gave up all pretense of being calm.

"Mom! Dad! Something happened to Pasha!" she wailed.

"All right, honey. You're doing all the

right things." Her dad took over. He bent down and swiftly ran his hand down the injured pony's back leg. Pasha flinched and tremors ran over her chestnut coat. "I hope it's just a sprain and not a torn ligament."

A torn ligament was serious. A feeling of dread jolted through Alex as she saw her parents exchanging serious looks. She'd had Pasha for three years and loved her to pieces. She couldn't bear to think of the plucky little chestnut pony being in pain.

A voice came over the loudspeaker. "Vet to show jumping, please. Right away."

It seemed like hours before the van arrived and the vet was examining Pasha with her expert eye. Alex stood with her arms around her pony's warm neck, trying hard not to cry. "Don't be scared, Pasha.

The vet's a nice lady. She's going to help you," she said gently.

Mrs. Judd put a hand on her daughter's arm. "Why don't you go and wait with Zoe, sweetie? She looks worried sick for you over there. We'll take care of Pasha. I'll come get you the moment the vet's finished."

Alex didn't want to leave Pasha, but she nodded miserably. She walked over to her best friend who was standing a few feet away with Maxi, her brown-and-white Welsh pony.

Zoe looked close to tears, too. "Poor Pasha. What a terrible thing to happen. Is she going to be okay?" she asked.

"I don't know. The vet's still examining her." Alex gulped, grateful that Zoe was there. They lived a few

miles away from each other up at Denton
Moor and had known each other since
they were little. They were both crazy
about ponies and did everything together.

Alex swallowed, blinking away unshed
tears. A horrible thought dawned on her.
"Was . . . was it my fault? I'm not as good
at jumping as you are. I . . . I might have
done something wrong that made Pasha
land awkwardly."

Zoe shook her head. "I don't think so.
Everything looked fine from where I was."

Alex nodded slowly, hoping that Zoe was right and not just saying that to make her feel better.

The wait was almost unbearable, but eventually the vet was finished. The moment the vet dusted off her hands and rose to her feet, Alex rushed back.

"What's wrong with Pasha? Her leg's not broken, is it? She's not going to have to be . . ." She couldn't say the awful words.

"No," the vet said quickly, banishing Alex's worst fears. "But it's a bad sprain and she split her heel. Your pony's going to be out of action for some time while she rests that leg."

Alex was so relieved that Pasha wasn't more seriously hurt that it took a few seconds for the news to sink in. "But . . .

she is going to get all better?"

The vet nodded. "There's no reason why she shouldn't make a full recovery. I gave her some medicine, so she'll be more comfortable on the trip home."

Alex felt faint with relief. She turned and gave Zoe a thumbs-up. Zoe waved back, beaming.

With the vet and her dad helping, they managed to get Pasha safely up the ramp and into their truck. The big horse truck wasn't new when they got it recently, and there was a dent on one side. Inside, it had room for four ponies and lots of space for equipment.

Once Pasha was tethered in her stall, Alex gave her a handful of oats. "You were so brave," she crooned, patting her. "Take a nice nap now."

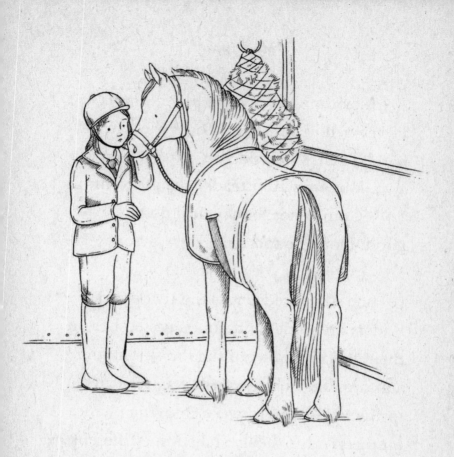

Back outside, she didn't know what
to do. Zoe was grooming Maxi and
her mom was making lunch. Her dad
suggested they take a walk around the
show's booths, which sold everything
from riding boots to the latest saddle soap.

Alex didn't really feel like it. Pasha's injury had cast a shadow over the day for her. "Thanks, but do you mind if I go for a walk by myself instead?" she asked him.

"'Course not, honey. It'll do you good. Don't be too long."

"I won't."

She wandered across the truck park. Riders on ponies and horses passed her on their way to and from the show-jumping and dressage enclosures. It was a warm spring day; families were enjoying picnics on the grass as they watched the different competitions.

Alex went through a gateway that led to a small wooded area. Flame-shaped yellow crocuses glowed against the dark soil next to shy violets. One or two people were walking their dogs, but the

place was mostly empty. The rich smells
of bark and grass surrounded her.

Alex paused on the shore of a small
lake. She noticed a patch of mist hovering
above the water. It seemed to be drifting
toward her.

Suddenly there was a bright flash
of violet sparkles, and a shimmering

cloud filled the entire clearing. Alex saw rainbow droplets glistening on her skin.

"Oh!" She narrowed her eyes, trying to peer through the strange multicolored mist.

As it began to fade, Alex saw that a pony was walking toward her. It was a palomino with a glossy caramel-colored coat, a sandy mane and tail, and bright deep-violet eyes.

"Can you help me, please?" it asked in a velvety neigh.

Chapter
TWO

Alex froze. She stared at the pretty pony in complete astonishment. She must still be feeling so upset about poor Pasha that she was imagining things! Whoever heard of a pony that could talk?

"What are you doing in here? I wonder who you belong to," she murmured aloud to herself.

The pony lifted its head proudly and

flared its nostrils. "I belong to no one. I am
Comet of the Lightning Herd. I have just
arrived here from far away."

Alex's jaw dropped. "Y-you can talk?
B-but how come?"

"All the magical Lightning Horses in
my herd can talk," Comet told her. "What
is your name?"

Alex swallowed, still not quite believing
that this was happening. She felt like she'd
stumbled into a real live fairy tale.

"I-I'm . . . um, Alexandra Judd, but everyone calls me Alex," she found herself stammering. "I'm . . . here at the horse show with my parents and my best friend, Zoe . . ."

Comet dipped his head in a formal bow, and his pale sandy mane swung forward. "I am honored to meet you, Alex."

"Um . . . me too," Alex said, feeling as if she should curtsy or something. "Did you say that you came from far away? Like a different country?"

"Much farther. I live in another world on Rainbow Mist Island with my twin sister, Destiny."

"Really? Wow! Is she here, too? Where is she?" Alex asked, fascinated, looking around for another talking palomino.

Comet shook his head. "Destiny is here in your world, but she is in hiding. She fled here after the Stone of Power was lost during our game of cloud-racing. The stone protects our herd from the dark horses who want to steal our magic. It has been found, but Destiny does not know this. I have come to find her and take her home."

Alex blinked at the handsome pony. What he had told her was so magical and strange. She wasn't sure that she could take it all in. But one thing in particular was puzzling her.

"Cloud-racing? What's—" she began.

Comet's violet eyes widened. "Stay back, please," he snorted.

Alex felt a strange tingling sensation flowing down to her fingertips as violet sparks ignited in Comet's caramel-colored coat and shimmering rainbow mist swirled around him. The palomino had disappeared, and in its place was a pale-cream pony with a flowing gold mane and tail that sparkled like spun silk. But it was the wide gold-feathered wings springing from his shoulders that stole Alex's breath.

"Oh!" She gasped in utter amazement at the incredible sight. Nothing could have prepared her for anything so beautiful. "Comet?"

"Yes. It is still me, Alex. Do not be alarmed," Comet said in a deep velvety whinny.

Before Alex had time to get used to seeing Comet in his true form, there was another spurt of violet sparkles and the multicolored mist broke into shining dust and disappeared, revealing the palomino pony once more.

"That's an amazing disguise! Can Destiny make herself look like a normal pony, too?"

Comet nodded, his ears swiveling. "But her disguise will not protect her if the dark horses find her. I must search for my sister. Will you help me?"

"Of course I will," Alex said, even though she had no idea where to look. "Do you think Destiny might be here at the horse show?"

Comet twitched his sandy tail. "I cannot sense that she is near. We will need to look for her on the slopes and hills nearby."

"It's pretty wild up in the high fields. There are tons of places among the rocks and caves where Destiny could hide," Alex said thoughtfully. "I'll be going home to Scarp Hill Farm in a few hours. I could ask Mom and Dad if you could come with me. We're used to taking care of animals. There's lots of room in our horse truck, even with two ponies in it already. That's Pasha, my pony. She just hurt herself," she said, feeling a ripple of anxiety. She dragged her attention back to the magic pony. "And . . . and Maxi, who belongs to Zoe, my best friend. I can't wait to see everyone's faces when I tell them about you!"

"No! You cannot tell anyone my secret," Comet neighed, his violet eyes serious. "You must promise me, Alex."

Alex pressed her lips together. She felt disappointed that she couldn't tell her parents about the amazing pony. But it seemed even worse to keep secrets from Zoe. They usually told each other everything.

She nodded slowly. "Well—okay . . . ," she said, prepared to agree if it would keep Comet and Destiny safe from their enemies.

Comet reached out to bump his nose gently against her arm. "Thank you."

"No problem!" Alex smiled and reached up to stroke him. She rubbed between his eyes, feeling proud that he had chosen her for his friend.

"I will come to your home. It will be a safe place to stay," Comet neighed.

"Cool! I'd *really* love that. But how am I going to explain about you and where you suddenly came from . . ."

"There you are!" called a voice.

Alex spun around to see Zoe running up to her. "Your mom sent me to find you. Lunch is ready . . . wow! Who does that gorgeous pony belong to?"

"What pony?" Alex asked, too flustered to think straight.

"Du-uh! The palomino standing right there in front of you!" Zoe pointed at Comet.

"Oh, *that* pony. Well . . . he's . . . um . . ." Alex fumbled for an explanation before an idea suddenly came to her. "I . . . er, found him running loose. He probably belongs to someone at the horse show."

Alex knew that if she reported Comet no one would be missing this magic pony! They'd probably assume that his owner had left without him, and her mom and dad definitely wouldn't mind looking after Comet while they waited for him to be claimed.

Comet nuzzled Alex's shoulder in gratitude for not giving away his special secret. "Thank you, Alex."

Alex gasped. Comet had just spoken— in front of Zoe! What could he be thinking?

But her friend appeared not to have noticed anything odd. It was very strange.

Alex tried to get ahold of herself. She told Zoe that she had found him loose in the woods. "I managed to catch him and calm him down. The owner's probably going crazy looking for him," she said, hoping that she sounded convincing.

"How awful to lose your pony!" Zoe exclaimed. "I'd be so upset if Maxi got loose and ran off. Comet? That's a cool name. How do you know that's what he's called?"

"I don't," Alex said. "I . . . just thought I'd call him that. He looks like a comet, with his pale mane and tail."

"It's a great name. It really suits him," Zoe said. "I'll come with you and help find his owner. Hold on—I'll go get a

halter and lead rope."

As Zoe dashed off to the horse truck, Alex looked at Comet. "I almost lost it when you spoke in front of her! How come she didn't seem to hear you?"

Comet's eyes gleamed. "I used my magic so that only you will be able to hear me. To anyone else I will seem like a normal pony."

Alex grinned at her special new friend. Comet was anything but normal!

Chapter
THREE

As the horse truck trundled up the steep road that led to the fields, Alex glanced into the back happily. Three sets of pricked ponies' ears were visible: Pasha's, Maxi's—and Comet's.

Alex hadn't even needed to beg her mom and dad to let Comet come home with them. One look at the handsome palomino, and Mrs. Judd had fallen in love with him—just as Alex had—and practically insisted they take care of Comet until his owner showed up.

Despite her injury, Pasha stood quietly munching hay in the partition next to Comet. It was as if the magic pony's presence had a calming influence on the chestnut pony.

Mr. Judd stopped the truck in front of Zoe's house, a rambling stone cottage called Gray Lag House.

Zoe's dad came out and greeted them cheerily. He helped Alex's dad let down the ramp and lead Maxi into the yard. Zoe carried her brown-and-white gelding's equipment to the stable.

"Thanks very much for taking us with you," she called to Alex's parents. She turned to Alex. "I'll ride over tomorrow morning for some jumping practice. Oh, I forgot—there's no point now, with poor Pasha being hurt, right?"

"I guess not." Alex's spirits sank as she thought how boring school break would be without riding with her best friend. She brightened as a thought came to her. "Wait a minute! I'll need to exercise Comet, so I may as well ride him while Pasha's getting better."

Comet nickered agreement from inside the truck.

"That sounds like the perfect arrangement," Alex's mom said. "Finding Comet running loose like that seems to have turned out to be a stroke of luck."

"Definitely! I'm going to take the best care of him!" Alex said with a wide

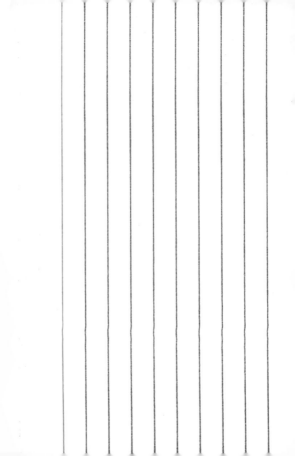

grin. "I'll see you tomorrow then!" She waved to her friend as they drove down the track and headed home to Scarp Hill Farm.

Alex was so eager to ride the magic pony that it made her pulse race. She hoped Pasha wouldn't be jealous.

Early the following morning, Alex went to check that her chestnut pony was comfortable. "Hello there, brave girl," she crooned, sliding open the door to Pasha's stall. When she'd settled her in last night, she'd been careful to pile up clean straw extra high around the walls to make a deep and comfortable bed.

Pasha was lying down. She lifted her head and looked at Alex with mild eyes. Alex sat down and gently rubbed her soft

brown nose. "That's right. You just relax
and let that bad old leg get better. The
vet's coming to check on you again later."

From the next stall, Comet gave a
soft whicker of encouragement. Pasha
nickered back softly and then lay down
with a contented sigh. Alex gave her a
final pat and made sure she had food and
water. Then she fed Comet and started
her usual stable chores.

She suddenly felt a strange warm tingling sensation in her fingertips as bright violet sparks ignited in Comet's caramel coat. His ears crackled with tiny rainbow bolts of magical power. Her eyes widened. What was going on?

She watched in total amazement as there was a whooshing noise and thousands of tiny fireflies shot into the air. *Swoosh! Rustle! Shine!* They rushed about swiftly scooping up soiled straw and dropping it into a wheelbarrow, and busily cleaning and polishing the bridles hanging on a nearby hook.

Alex stood by, her hands at her sides, feeling a bit uncomfortable as there was nothing for her to do. Soon all the work was done. The glittery helpers dissolved into sparkly dust and disappeared. Alex

took a deep breath as she realized there
was something she had to get straight.

"Thanks so much for helping me,
Comet. But I really don't mind doing
this work," she said tactfully. "Actually,
I enjoy it. It's all part of looking after a
pony."

"I did not think of that. Thank you
for explaining. I will ask if you need help
next time," Comet neighed.

Alex smiled, glad that her magical

friend understood and she hadn't hurt his feelings. "Zoe will be here soon. Dad said we could practice jumping in the field. It's going to be fun. Maxi's pretty good. But I've got a feeling that you're going to be even better."

Comet snorted happily as she led him out of the stable into the yard. "I like Zoe and Maxi."

Alex had just finished tacking him up and was tightening the girth around his tummy when she heard hoofbeats. She whirled around with an eager smile and saw two riders coming up the winding lane toward the farm.

She frowned. "That's strange. Who's that with Zoe? Oh, it's her cousin Saffron," she said, her spirits sinking.

"You do not sound pleased," said Comet.

"It's just that I was looking forward to having fun today with you, Zoe, and Maxi," Alex admitted. "It won't be the same with Saffron. Oh well, she's here now. I guess it will be okay. It won't be for that long."

Comet looked up curiously as the two girls trotted through the farm gate.

Zoe stood up in her stirrups and waved. "Hi, Alex! Guess what? My aunt and uncle and Saffron have come to stay with me for the school break. She can practice jumping with us."

"Oh, okay." Alex tried not to sound too rude but still felt a prickle of dismay at the thought of having to share her best friend for two whole weeks. Saffron was older than both of them. Alex had only met her once before, and she didn't know her all that well.

"Hi, Alex." Zoe's twelve-year-old cousin sat on a flashy pony. She wore pink-and-black gloves that matched her stylish riding helmet. Her saddle cloth had her name on it in glittery writing.

"Hi, Saffron." Alex forced a smile, making an effort to be friendly. "Your pony's really pretty. What's her name?"

"Sparkly Fairy Princess," Saffron said.

"Oh . . . okay. Cool." But despite the fussy name, the gray pony was really

beautiful, with an elegant head and large dark eyes. Her silvery mane flopped prettily over her forehead.

"Zoe told me what happened at the horse show. That's too bad about Pasha."

"Yeah. It was pretty awful. The vet says she'll be okay, though," Alex told her."That's good. It's horrible when your pony's hurt." Saffron ran her eyes over Comet. "That palomino you're taking care of seems friendly. What's he like to ride?"

"I haven't had a chance to find out yet. His name is Comet, by the way," Alex told her. "I'll be riding him for the first time today."

Saffron nodded. "It's always exciting to ride a new pony, isn't it?"

"Yes." Alex thought Saffron seemed

confident, but also quite friendly. Maybe having her around wouldn't be so bad, after all.

"Saffron's going to give us some neat jumping tips. She really knows her stuff. Uncle Tim's won tons of competitions," Zoe said, smiling.

Alex remembered that Saffron's dad was Tim Hall-Chapman, a top show jumper.

"Yeah! Trust me, by the time I've finished putting you two through your paces, you'll be jumping like professionals," Saffron said, with a determined glint in her eye.

"Um . . . good." Alex's smile wavered a bit. She wasn't sure whether Zoe's cousin meant that as a promise or a threat.

Chapter
FOUR

"No, not like that! Do it like *this*!"
Saffron instructed bossily, waving her
arms as Alex assembled the last jump.
"Hurry up!"

Alex sighed. It had taken the three
girls over an hour to set up the course of
jumps in the field. And Saffron had found
fault with every one of them.

Alex bit back a rude comment as she

repositioned the poles for the third time. Finally, the last fence was in place and Saffron gave her a thumbs-up.

"I'm surprised she didn't want me to get a ruler to measure the jumps, too," she complained to Comet in a whisper. "Anyone would think this was a perfectly fine show-jumping arena!"

Comet's sandy mane stirred in the cool breeze. "Saffron seems to want everything just right."

"Tell me about it!" Alex grumbled as she mounted the magic pony.

On the ride back down the field to Zoe and Saffron, Alex's mood lightened. Comet was wonderful to ride. She loved the way he moved with a smooth stride, arching his supple neck and holding his head high.

When she stopped next to Zoe and
Maxi, the big brown-and-white pony
turned his head toward Comet and gave
a friendly blow. The two ponies were
already getting along well.

Alex took a deep breath. "Okay.
We're finally ready. Who wants to go—"
she began.

"Me first!" Saffron was already urging
the gray pony forward. She and Princess
streaked toward the first fence.

"She's pretty eager, isn't she?" Zoe said admiringly, gazing at her cousin.

"That's one way of putting it," Alex murmured.

They watched as Saffron handled Princess expertly and sailed over all the fences. The gray pony trotted back to them with her ears pricked.

"Way to go!" Zoe cried. "That was great!"

"Well done, Saffron!" Alex added. She had to admit that Saffron was an amazing rider.

Saffron made a face. "Those little jumps are easy-peasy! Princess could almost step over them. We're used to much more challenging ones," she boasted.

They might be little but they're the best we've got! Alex thought, a bit annoyed,

especially after all the fuss Saffron had
made about getting them just right.
Besides, her dad had gone to a lot of
trouble to gather together the poles
and other props so they could have fun
jumping.

Zoe went next. Alex and Saffron sat
side by side, watching and calling out
encouragement from where they sat on
their ponies.

As Maxi cantered toward a fence,
Alex noticed that Zoe was leaning a little
too far forward.

Saffron saw it as well. Her voice
suddenly boomed out. "For goodness'
sake, sit up straight. And keep your hands
and heels down!"

Zoe jerked on the reins and almost
jumped out of her skin. Maxi stepped

sideways and crashed into the fence,
knocking down a pole.

Alex rode toward her. "Is Maxi
okay?" she asked worriedly. "I hope he
didn't hurt himself."

Zoe dismounted and checked her
pony's knees and legs. "He seems fine,"
she said.

Saffron looked down from Princess.

"Why didn't you do what I told you?"
she demanded.

Alex began helping Zoe rebuild the
fence. "You'd probably have been all
right if Saffron hadn't yelled at you like
that," she sympathized. "It put you off
your stride."

Saffron's brows dipped in a fierce
frown. "What's the big deal? I was only
trying to help! It's not my fault if she
didn't listen!"

"Well, maybe if you didn't shout like
a foghorn—" Alex began.

"It doesn't matter now," Zoe cut in
hastily. "I'll do better next time. Your
turn, Alex." She mounted Maxi and then
she and Saffron trotted away together to
watch.

Alex clicked her tongue at Comet,

and he sprang toward the first fence. He cleared it easily, arching his neck and proudly tossing his mane. Alex could tell he was enjoying himself.

Comet soared over all the fences in turn, until there was just one left. They were approaching the final fence when Alex had a sudden flashback to the recent horse show where Pasha was injured.

As the chestnut's frightened whinny seemed to ring in her head, Alex felt her confidence waver. Maybe she was doing something wrong when she jumped, despite what Zoe thought. Could it have been her fault that Pasha had hurt herself?

She gulped. *What if Comet lands wrong and hurts himself, too?*

The magic pony slowed down. Alex's mouth dried as she tried to force down her fear and work through it. Comet got slower still. He was going to refuse!

"Stop hesitating!" Saffron shouted loudly. "Kick him on. Show him who's boss!"

Alex flushed with annoyance, but managed to get her focus back. She swallowed hard. "Come on, Comet!" she whispered, pressing him on.

Comet sped up again. He eyed the fence carefully and bounded over it easily.

"Good job!" Alex gasped as they landed safely.

"Are you all right, Alex?" Comet champed at the bit. "It felt like you didn't really want me to jump. I didn't want to go over it if you were frightened."

She leaned down to rub his silky caramel neck. "I did get scared for a

moment when I remembered how Pasha
got hurt the last time I was jumping. I
thought I might have done something
wrong that time, and I didn't want you to
get hurt, too."

Comet turned his head and blew air
out of his flared nostrils. "That was not
your fault. Pasha told me on the journey
to your home that she had slipped on a
patch of mud. It was an accident."

"Really?" Alex said as relief flowed

through her. "Thanks, Comet. It's great to know that for sure." She felt a surge of affection for her magic friend as they rode over to Zoe and Saffron.

"That last jump was really messy," Saffron criticized. "To be a good show jumper, you have to keep your mind on what you're doing. Otherwise you won't get anywhere!"

Alex reacted without thinking. "So I lost concentration for a minute. It's not a crime, is it?" she said sharply.

"I was only saying," Saffron said huffily. "Some people are so touchy!"

There was an awkward silence.

Alex saw that Zoe's face had clouded with embarrassment and immediately wished that she'd bitten her tongue. "Sorry. I didn't mean to snap," she apologized. "I guess I'm still a bit worried about Pasha's bad leg."

Saffron shrugged. "If you say so. My turn again." She urged her pony forward. "Come on, Princess! Let's show them how it's done! Watch and learn, you two amateurs!"

Alex tried to suppress a flicker of irritation. "Why does she have to be so bossy all the time? I thought this was supposed to be fun," she whispered to Comet.

But she must have spoken more loudly that she'd intended because Zoe heard her.

"Saffron can't help being competitive," she said, defending her cousin. "Wouldn't you be if your dad expected you to follow in his footsteps and be a top show jumper? Uncle Tim's nice, but he's really strict. Give her a chance, Alex. She's okay when you get to know her better."

Alex wisely kept quiet. She didn't actually want to get to know Saffron better.

Why can't it just be me and Comet and Zoe and Maxi for the school break? Like we'd planned, she thought wistfully.

"Anyway, we all need to work extra hard if we're going to try out for the jumping show at the Pony Club fund-raising event in two weeks," Zoe was saying.

Alex blinked at her. "The what?"

"I was going to tell you. Saffron entered all three of us. It's a special surprise."

Alex was stunned. "She could have asked if we even wanted to try out for it!"

Zoe started grinning. "Duh! Then it wouldn't have been a surprise, would it, you silly goose?" she teased.

"I guess not." Alex felt a smile beginning to surface. It was the first time today that she and Zoe had laughed together. It felt good—like old times, when it was just the two of them.

"Clear around—again—for the marvelously talented Saffron Hall–Chapman on the wonderful Sparkly Fairy Princess!" The over-the-top voice echoed around the field as if it were coming out of a loudspeaker at a horse event.

Zoe was giggling as she rode over to her cousin. "You're a riot, Saffron!"

It was actually pretty funny. Despite herself, Alex managed a smile. She still thought that Zoe's cousin was the bossiest girl she'd ever met, though. How was she going to get along with her for two whole weeks?

But as she wound Comet's thick mane through her fingers, Alex felt herself calming down. She thought she could probably put up with anything,

even Zoe's pushy cousin, as long as she
had Comet. He was her own wonderful
secret, never to be shared with anyone.

"I think you deserve a treat, Comet!"
Dismounting, she fished in her pocket
for a packet of mints and held them up to
him in the palm of her hand. She smiled

as the palomino's soft lips nuzzled her hand as he snuffled them up.

"Delicious!" He crunched them, spraying bits everywhere and making Alex laugh.

Chapter
FIVE

Alex fought back tears the following day. She and her mom stood in the yard, watching the horse ambulance disappear down the winding lane.

A different vet had just come over to check Pasha's leg. He suspected there might be complications, so the pony was being taken to a special treatment center.

"Pasha won't like being away from

her own stable. She's going to miss having her cuddle when I settle her for the night." Alex gulped.

"Try not to worry about her, honey," Mrs. Judd said gently. "Pasha's in very good hands."

"I know, but I can't help it. I'm really going to miss her."

"'Course you will. That's normal. So will I." Her mom gave her a hug. After

a while she said, "Are you hanging out with Zoe and Saffron today?"

Alex shook her head. "They're going out for the day with Zoe's aunt and uncle. But we're meeting up here tomorrow so we can do some more jumping. I thought I might go out for a ride in the fields by myself," Alex told her.

"Good idea. That'll take your mind off things."

Mrs. Judd stood by as Alex tacked up Comet and then mounted him. As she rode out into the yard, her mom reached up and patted the palomino pony's neck.

"Look after her, won't you, boy? She's my special girl."

Comet whickered softly and pricked his ears.

"I could swear he understands

everything you say to him," her mom
said, smiling.

Alex smiled back. "He does!" *If only
Mom knew.*

"See you later!" called Mrs. Judd
over her shoulder as she went toward the
farmhouse.

"Bye!" Alex answered.

As they trotted out of the yard, she
spoke to Comet. "Destiny might be
hiding among the rocks and crags. We
can search for her."

His sandy tail flicked up. "Thank
you, Alex."

At the end of the winding lane, Alex
pointed him toward one of the stony
tracks that led up to the high fields. Soon
they found themselves in a stark landscape
under huge open skies.

Alex loved it up there. Drystone walls
snaked across the hillside, where sheep
and their lambs grazed on the scrubby
grass. Here and there, enormous jagged
gray stones thrust upward from the bare
soil like sleeping giants. Some of them
were grouped together, forming natural
shelters and hiding places.

"Hold tight!" Comet shot forward
like a rocket, and Alex felt a glow of
excitement.

Tiny rainbows glimmered in his
mane as his shining hooves ate up the
ground. She felt a warm tingling feeling
flow to the ends of her fingertips and his
magic swirled around her, keeping her
safe as they galloped as fast as the wind.
She knew that she'd never get tired of
riding the magic pony.

"Yea! Go, Comet, go!" she shouted,
her voice ringing out across the expanse
of the fields.

Comet raked the landscape with his
keen eyes, looking for any signs of his
lost twin. Alex kept her eyes peeled,
too. They explored the rock formations
and hidden spaces. But all they saw
were three walkers climbing a hill and
a farmer on a tractor checking his flock.

There was no sign of any ponies.

The ground sloped gradually upward, and the soil became thin and stony. Pink and purple heather clothed the ground and grew in cracks in the stones. Comet galloped on tirelessly, but they found no trace of Destiny.

Alex suggested that they search lower down among the winding lanes and farm buildings. The sun came out, turning Comet's caramel coat and sandy mane and tail to molten gold. Cloud shadows rippled across the sloping hills.

Suddenly, Comet stiffened. Catching a movement from the corner of his eye, he laid back his ears.

"What's wrong?" she asked him.

"A dark horse is close!" he neighed in panic.

Alex couldn't see anything but before she could catch her breath, Comet bolted straight for a gap in a broken wooden fence. He was going to barge through it!

Alex caught sight of the dull sheen of metal. There was barbed wire strung across the gap, but Comet hadn't noticed.

"Stop!" she cried, pulling on the reins.

But Comet pounded on, blinded by his terror of the enemy horses from his world who wanted to steal his power. The dangerous fence was right in front of them!

One step. Two steps. Three . . .

In desperation, Alex pulled at the reins. "Stop, Comet!" she begged. "There's nothing there!"

It did the trick. Comet came to his

senses. But he stopped so suddenly that
Alex lost her balance. She flew forward
right over his head and crashed into the
fence.

The fence's rotten wood collapsed
beneath her, breaking her fall. "Oh!" she
gasped as the barbed wire tore into her
jeans and pain shot through her leg.

Biting her lip, she tore herself free
and stumbled to her feet. She limped
toward Comet, desperate to make sure
he was all right.

The magic pony's sides were heaving,
and he sucked air noisily through his
flared nostrils.

"It's okay. You're safe," Alex soothed
gently. "It was only a trick of the light
from the shadows moving across the hills."

Gradually, Comet grew calm.

"You risked yourself to save me.
Thank you, Alex," he whickered fondly,
lowering his head to gently nudge her
arm.

"Anyone would have done the same
thing," she said, cupping his velvety nose.

"No, they would not. You are a very
special friend, Alex."

A soft cloud of his warm hay-scented
breath enveloped her, and Alex's heart
swelled with love for her magic pony.
She reached up and put her arms around

Comet's neck. Closing her eyes, she pressed her cheek to his silky warmth. After a few moments of wonderful closeness that she would never forget, she drew back.

"Mom will have lunch ready. We'd better go . . . oh!" She winced. Now that the excitement was over, her injured leg began to throb horribly.

Comet's eyes widened with concern. "You are hurt! I will help you!"

Alex felt another tingling sensation flowing down to her fingertips as violet sparks bloomed in Comet's caramel coat and a glittering mist filled with hundreds of tiny stars rose into the air. It floated down and surrounded her leg, where it swirled briefly before sinking into her torn jeans and disappearing.

The sharp pain seemed to melt away

like the morning mist in the fields. As Alex watched, the edges of her ripped jeans drew together and fixed themselves.

"Thanks, Comet! I feel much better now."

Comet swiveled his ears. "You're welcome. Climb back on my back, Alex. Let us return."

Alex did so. Thorn bushes and stone walls sped past, and soon they were approaching the winding lane that led to Scarp Hill Farm. Comet gave an excited neigh as he slowed to a halt. Stretching out his neck, he looked at the ground.

Alex peered over his shoulder to see what he was looking at.

She did a double take.

Stretching ahead of them and curving away out of sight behind a nearby

farmyard was a faint line of softly glowing
violet hoofprints.

"What's that?" Alex asked in wonder.

"It's Destiny's trail! She has been
here!" Comet told her.

Alex gasped. Did that mean that
the magic pony was leaving—right

now—to go after his twin? "Is . . . is she somewhere close?" she asked him anxiously.

"No. This trail is cold. But at least I know that Destiny came this way. When I am closer to her I will sense her presence and hear her hoofbeats."

"Will I be able to hear them, too?" she asked, starting to relax a bit.

"Yes, if you are riding me or we are close together. But other humans will not be able to hear them." His glowing eyes grew serious. "I may have to leave suddenly, without saying good-bye, to catch up with Destiny."

Alex fought against a new feeling of dismay. She didn't think she would ever be ready to lose her friend. "Once . . . once you find her, you could both stay

here with me, couldn't you?" she asked
hopefully in a wobbly voice.

Comet shook his head. "I am afraid
that is not possible. We must return to
our family on Rainbow Mist Island. I
hope you understand, Alex."

Alex nodded sadly. She swallowed
hard as she tried not to think about
Comet leaving and promised herself
that she was going to enjoy every single
moment spent with him.

Chapter SIX

"Ta-da! How about that for a water jump?" Alex said with a proud flourish.

She was in the lower field with Zoe and Saffron and their ponies. There was a large muddy puddle at the bottom of a slope. Earlier, her dad had helped her position a row of logs along its shortest side.

"Perfect!" Zoe said, smiling.

Saffron shrugged, unimpressed.
"It's not bad, I suppose." Her matching
helmet, gloves, and designer jacket were
the color of limes today, and she held a
dainty little riding whip.

Alex felt conscious of her muddy
boots, old jeans, and battered body
warmer. She was glad that Zoe was
dressed in similar practical clothes.

They all lined up at the water jump.
Zoe and Maxi went first. The brown-

and-white pony landed well, picking up his feet as he cantered onto dry grass.

Alex went next: Comet jumped perfectly, leaping over the logs and splashing through the water. He even bucked playfully when he'd finished.

Alex laughed aloud. To herself she murmured, *Find fault with that, if you can, Saffron.*

Princess, on the other hand, obviously didn't want to get wet. As Saffron rode her toward the logs, the gray pony suddenly stopped. Taken by surprise, Saffron almost lost her balance. She only just managed to stay in her saddle as Princess stuck her nose in the air and pranced cheekily around the puddle.

Zoe and Alex laughed at the pony's antics.

Saffron flushed bright red. "Come on, Princess. Stop misbehaving!" Pressing her lips together, she lined her pony up again.

Princess champed at the bit, threw up her head, and slowed down, about to refuse again. Saffron gave her a light tap on her back with the whip. The gray pony sprang over the log from a standing position and stopped dead in the middle of the puddle.

Alex was helpless with laughter. Princess was really putting on a show today.

Comet whickered, rolling back his lips as if he were laughing, too.

But Saffron was furious. "What's wrong with you?" she grumbled to her pony. "You're making me look really stupid!"

"Why don't you just try talking to her gently while you squeeze her on?" Alex suggested reasonably.

"I know what I'm doing! Dad's shown me how to deal with a stubborn pony!" Saffron retorted. She hit her pony on the back, but Princess still refused to move.

"I'd like to see how Saffron would

like it if someone hit her!" Alex whispered angrily to Comet. "Maybe someone should grab that whip!"

The magic pony's deep-violet eyes glowed with purpose.

Alex felt a familiar tingling sensation flow down to her fingertips as Comet opened his mouth and huffed out a large breath, which turned into a tiny violet fireball. It shot invisibly toward Saffron and Princess trailing tiny bright stars. The fireball burst above them, showering them with violet glitter before dissolving harmlessly. Saffron gasped with surprise as the dainty riding whip flew out of her hand, whizzed through the air and landed two feet away.

At the same time, Princess lowered her head and began pawing at the water.

Saffron was still looking at where the whip had landed and didn't seem to have noticed, but Zoe read the telltale signs.

"Oh no! Princess is going to roll! Watch out, Saffron!" she warned her cousin.

But it was too late. The gray pony sank to her knees as she lowered herself into the puddle.

"Ooh! Er!" Saffron lost her balance. She slipped forward, did an impressive somersault, and landed on her butt. As Princess rolled over, a wave of muddy water sloshed all over Saffron, soaking her from head to toe.

Princess stood up, shook herself, and calmly trotted to dry land.

Alex clapped her hands over her mouth. "Oh my goodness," she said in a muffled voice, trying without success to stop the laughter that was bubbling up inside her. "I didn't expect that to happen."

Her magical friend blinked at her with surprised long-lashed eyes. "I thought that was what you wanted."

Zoe dismounted and ran to help her cousin. "Are you okay?"

"Does it look like it?" Saffron burst into tears. "My clothes are ruined! They were a birthday present." Dripping, she

plodded through the mud and stopped in the field.

Seeing that Saffron was really upset, Alex abruptly stopped laughing. She felt an uncomfortable stirring of guilt.

Comet had only used his magic because she had grumbled to him about Saffron. Alex chewed at her lip, wondering what she could do to set things right.

Saffron had caught up with Princess. She grasped her bridle in a muddy hand. "Dad's going to be really mad if I take her back looking like this. She's filthy!" she wailed.

"Don't worry. I'll tell Uncle Tim it was an accident," Zoe said.

"It won't make any difference. He'll still blame me. You know how strict he is. He's got this saying: 'It's always the rider's fault.'"

"But that's not fair!" Alex exclaimed.

Unexpectedly, she felt herself starting to feel sorry for the older girl. It couldn't be much fun having a dad who was so strict. She thought hard and a plan began to form in her mind.

"I have an idea. Let's go to my house . . ."

Chapter SEVEN

"Oh, dear!" Mrs. Judd exclaimed when she saw Saffron standing miserably in the mud room, dripping mud and water everywhere.

To Alex's relief, her mom didn't waste time asking for explanations.

Mrs. Judd rolled up her sleeves. "Okay. Let's get you out of those wet clothes and into the shower. Alex, can you get me—"

"Sorry, Mom. I've got something super important to do," Alex interrupted swiftly. "Zoe will help. Won't you, Zoe?"

"Um . . . sure." Zoe frowned, puzzled.

"Towels are in the bathroom. And take any dry clothes from my bedroom," Alex called over her shoulder, dashing outside before anyone could protest.

She ran over to the stables where all three ponies were tethered. Comet whinnied a greeting when he saw her.

Alex looked at Princess in dismay.

The once elegant gray pony was covered with patches of smelly drying mud and streaked with grass stains. Her tangled mane and tail looked like frayed rope.

"Wow! She looks terrible, doesn't she?" Alex found herself wondering whether there would be time to put her plan into action. But she had to try.

First though, she had a confession to make to her magical friend.

"I'm . . . I'm sorry that I encouraged you to use your magic when I was upset. It was wrong of me, Comet. I know that now. Can you forgive me?"

"Of course. Everyone makes mistakes," the magic pony said. "It is what you do to fix them that is important."

Alex felt a bit better. "Thanks, Comet. You're the best. I've got an idea. This is how I can make it up to Saffron . . ."

The magic pony swiveled his ears and listened carefully as Alex told him what she had in mind. "But we'll have to hurry before Zoe, Saffron, or my mom come out here."

Comet nodded. "I will help you. But are you sure that this is what you want?" he asked, his eyes sparkling mischievously.

Alex didn't hesitate. "This time— definitely!"

She felt a familiar warm tingling sensation flowing down to the tips of her fingers. Large violet sparks ignited in Comet's caramel–colored coat, and a cloud of tiny bright lights like busy worker bees fluttered into the air. The glittering little helpers spread out, gathering everything they needed before they got to work. Alex watched in astonishment.

Splash! A hose sprayed warm soapy water over Princess, washing the mud from her coat, mane, and tail. *Swish!* Towels swept back and forth drying her. *Rustle!* Brushes buffed her coat, and combs gently untangled her mane and tail.

Princess sighed with contentment, enjoying being pampered. She even lifted each hoof in turn for it to be picked out, brushed, and oiled. Finally she was finished. Her coat gleamed like silver, and her mane and tail were brushed to a glossy silkiness.

"She looks wonderful. Thanks, Comet!"

"I am glad that I could help," Comet neighed as every last little glowing bee disappeared, and the deep-violet sparks faded from his coat.

They were only just in time. Zoe and Saffron were leaving the house and crossing the yard.

Saffron's eye widened when she saw Princess. "Alex? What . . . wow! I can't believe it!" she gasped delightedly. She was dressed in a pair of Alex's overalls and a spare pair of jodhpurs, which were tucked into a pair of her mom's old riding boots.

"How did you manage to get Princess looking like that?" Zoe asked.

You wouldn't believe me, even if I could tell you! she thought. "I love a challenge! Anyway, I didn't want to hang around and get bored, while everyone fussed over Saffron," she lied happily.

While Saffron was admiring her perfectly groomed pony, Zoe leaned close to whisper to Alex. "You can't fool me. You did it to stop Saffron from getting into trouble, didn't you?"

Alex shrugged. "Well, I did feel a bit sorry for her. I didn't want her to get in trouble with her dad." She would have loved to tell Zoe the truth, but she couldn't do that without giving away Comet's secret. She knew that she would never tell anyone about her magical friend.

Comet seemed to know what she was thinking. He tossed his head and gave a soft whicker of approval.

Saffron turned to Alex. "Thanks, Alex. I won't forget this," she said warmly. "I . . . I know I can be a pain. It's the way I am, but I don't mean anything by it. Friends, okay?"

Alex flushed. "I guess I haven't been that easy to get along with, either," she admitted honestly. "It'll be different from now on."

"Yeah!" Zoe did a little dance of triumph. "Does this mean we can all concentrate on having fun and getting

ready for the Pony Club fund-raising
event?"

"You bet!" Alex and Saffron
exclaimed happily.

Chapter EIGHT

Comet's warm magic swirled around Alex as they paused on the heathery hillside a week later. His sides were heaving after a thrilling gallop, and as he looked out across the wide expanse of the land, he caught his breath.

Alex relaxed in the saddle, full of the afterglow of another exciting ride on the magic pony. If she lived to be a hundred,

she would never forget the joy of riding him.

She had spent the afternoon at Zoe's house, watching some of Saffron's show-jumping DVDs. Zoe's mom had gotten pizza and snacks and turned the event into a party.

Now Alex and Comet were cutting across the fields on their way home.

Another search among the rock formations had proved fruitless. There had been no more signs of Destiny.

"It was so much fun today and Saffron was great. We're all getting along better. But Zoe will always be my best friend," Alex told him happily, resting her hands in her lap.

Comet huffed out a warm breath and snorted softly. "I am glad that things have worked out well for you."

Alex thought she detected a trace of sadness in his voice and guessed that he was missing his twin sister.

"They'll work out for you and Destiny, too," she said nicely. "I know they will."

Comet's eyes glowed with new hope. "I hope so. Thank you, Alex."

Gray clouds were gathering above the

huge boulders. Alex shivered and reached out to stroke the palomino's silky neck. "It's getting cold. There's a warm stable and a bucket of oats waiting for you at home. Shall we go?"

Comet pricked his ears. "I am ready. Hold tight!"

Alex caught her breath as the magic pony rocked back onto his hind legs and pawed the air with his hooves. When he leaped forward, tiny rainbows glimmered in his caramel coat and sandy mane.

They galloped toward a stony track and in no time at all reached the winding lane that led to Scarp Hill Farm. Comet smoothly changed pace, and Alex rose to the trot as the farmhouse came into view.

Her heart gave a lurch as she spotted a truck in the yard. It was the horse

ambulance. "Pasha's back from the
specialist center!" she cried delightedly.

Dismounting quickly, she led Comet
into the stable.

"Pasha!" The chestnut pony was in
her stall, which was open and led into the
yard. At the sound of Alex's voice, she
pricked her ears. Turning her head, she
nickered and gave a friendly blow. Comet
snorted softly to her and the ponies gently
touched noses.

"Oh, that's so sweet. Pasha looks a lot
happier, doesn't she?" Alex stroked her
pony's nose.

She quickly unsaddled the magic pony
and gave him a scoop of food to eat, before
rushing into the house to talk to her mom.

Simon Green, the vet, was sitting at
the table, drinking a cup of coffee. He

looked up and smiled. "Hi, Alex."

"Hi, Simon. Hi, Mom. I just saw Pasha! She looks great! Has the treatment worked? When can I exercise her on a lunge rope in the yard? How soon can I ride her again?" Eager questions spilled out of her.

"Slow down, honey!" Mrs. Judd cautioned. "I think you should listen to what Simon has to say before you get your hopes up. Isn't that right, Simon?"

The vet nodded. "The treatment she had was something very new, involving stem cells. It seemed to go well, but I'm afraid we can't expect miracles . . ."

Alex felt her high spirits sinking as she listened to Simon explaining that it could be weeks before they knew whether the treatment had worked. "Does . . . does that mean Pasha's leg might never get better?"

"I think there's a fair chance that it will. But it's best to be prepared just in case," came the vet's reply. "As I say, miracles are rare."

A fair chance? What did that mean? It didn't sound all that promising. Alex felt her hopes being crushed.

After Simon left, Alex went back out to the stable. She found Comet standing with his head very close to Pasha's. The little chestnut pony's eyes were closed and she had a blissful look on her face.

As Comet sensed Alex's presence, he looked up and stepped back from Pasha. His eyes glowed like amethysts. It was a look that sank deep inside her chest and made her heart flutter.

"Comet—" Alex began.

But before she could finish her question, Alex heard the sound that she had been hoping for and dreading at the same time: the hollow sound of galloping hooves overhead.

She froze. Destiny was here! There was no mistake.

Comet raced past her out of the stable.

Alex ran after him to a corner of the yard where a twinkling rainbow mist was drifting down. In the middle of it, Comet

stood in his true form, a palomino pony
no longer. Rainbow droplets gleamed
on his noble arched neck, cream coat,
and flowing golden mane and tail;
magnificent gold–feathered wings sprang
from his powerful shoulders.

"Comet!" Alex gasped. She had almost
forgotten how beautiful he was. "You . . .
you're leaving right now, aren't you?"

His wonderful violet eyes lost a little
of their brightness for a second. "I must.
If I am to catch Destiny and save her from
our enemies."

Alex's throat burned with tears. She
knew she had to find the courage to
let her friend go. She hurried toward
him. Leaning against Comet's glowing
shoulder, she rested her face against his
warm silken cheek.

"I'll never forget you," she murmured adoringly.

"I will not forget you, either, Alex. You have been a good friend," Comet neighed softly. He allowed her to hug him one last time and then gently backed away. "Farewell. Ride well and true," he said in a deep musical voice.

There was a final flash of violet light and a silent explosion of rainbow sparkles that floated down around Alex and tinkled like miniature bells as they hit the ground.

Comet spread his golden wings and soared upward. He faded and was gone.

Alex wiped away tears, hardly able to believe that everything had happened so quickly. Something lay in the yard. It was a single glittering gold wing feather.

Bending down, she picked it up. The
feather tingled against her fingers as it
faded to a cream color. Alex slipped it
into her pocket. She would always keep
the feather to remind herself of the magic

pony and the wonderful adventure they had shared.

As she turned back toward the stable, she heard a soft neigh. Her little chestnut pony came out and cantered around the yard in a perfect circle before walking toward her. *Look at me, I'm all well again*, she seemed to be saying.

"Pasha! You're not hurt anymore!" Alex gasped delightedly. A smile broke out on her face as she knew that this was Comet's final gift to her. "You were wrong, Simon. Miracles can happen . . . when you have a magic pony's help!"

Pasha nudged her arm gently and blew sweet breath onto her neck. Alex threw her arms around her pony's neck and breathed out a long sigh of perfect happiness.

"Thank you so much, Comet. Take
care. And I hope you and Destiny get
back safely to Rainbow Mist Island."

Read the first chapter of

Magic Ponies

A Twinkle of Hooves

Chapter ONE

"Bye, Alice! I hope you and Fleur will be really happy!" Steph Danes called, her voice catching. She waved to the six-year-old girl who sat in the front seat of the car parked outside her house.

"Thank you. We will!" The little girl waved back, her small face shining with happiness.

Steph's eyes pricked with tears as the

car and the horse trailer it was towing moved slowly away up Porlock Close. She watched until they were out of sight and then her face crumpled as she turned to her mom.

Mrs. Danes gave her daughter a hug and stroked her short fair hair. "Good job,

honey. I know it was hard for you to let Fleur go. But we don't have the room to keep a pony you won't be riding anymore."

"I know." Steph sighed, wiping her eyes. "And Fleur's going to a good home. Alice really seemed to love her, didn't she?"

Her mom nodded, smiling fondly. "All little girls love their very own first pony the best. You were Alice's age when we got Fleur. It's too bad that you've outgrown her, but it happens to everyone eventually."

Steph nodded. She knew her mom was right, but she was going to miss Fleur, her little chestnut Dartmoor pony, like crazy. They'd had so much fun together in the last three years. Steph was going to feel very lonely not seeing her every day.

Steph and her mom walked back into

the house together. It was hot in the kitchen with the bright sun pouring in through the open back door. Steph got them cold drinks from the fridge.

She stared into space as she drank, feeling sad. Saturdays were usually for riding, and then grooming Fleur until her chestnut coat gleamed.

"Do you want to clear out the stable?" Mrs. Danes asked. "You could practice what you learned at that workshop on stable management over spring break."

Steph had really enjoyed the workshop. She wanted to work with horses when she grew up. "I guess I could do that now," she answered, deciding to get the upsetting task of removing all traces of Fleur over and done with.

Steph went outside to the old garage

at the side of the house. Her dad had converted it into a stable when they'd had the driveway extended and a bigger garage built. As she forked up soiled bedding and began to wheel it away, she felt an overwhelming wave of sadness. Fleur wasn't even here to appreciate what she was doing.

What was Steph going to do now without her very own little pony to look after and love? She sighed heavily before giving the stable floor one last mopping, but as she did a car drove up the cul-de-sac and pulled into the driveway.

Her dad got out and walked around to her. "Hello, sweetie. Keeping busy?" he asked.

Steph nodded. "I'm almost done. It's horrible, though, without Fleur."

"It must be," Mr. Danes agreed
sympathetically. "We'll all miss her."
He gave her a hug. "I knew you'd
need cheering up, so I popped into the
new riding stables in the village. Judy
Marshall, the owner, says they aren't too
busy today. You can go right over and
have your pick of the ponies to ride."

Steph stared at him in surprise. How
could he even think that she'd want to
ride a pony she didn't know? It was far
too soon. She'd feel disloyal to Fleur.

"I don't really feel like it right now.
Maybe some other time," she murmured.

"I don't like to think of you sitting
around brooding," her dad said kindly.
"Why don't you give the new stables a
try? Riding's what you love doing the
most, after all, isn't it?" he asked gently.

"Well, yes—usually," Steph admitted. She still wasn't sure that this was a good idea, but her dad had gone out of his way to get her a ride and she didn't want to hurt his feelings. "I guess I could go over there and take a look."

"That's the spirit! Come on, grab your riding gear. I'll have a quick word with your mom. See you in the car."

Despite herself, Steph felt a bit brighter because of his enthusiasm. Maybe getting to know some new ponies would be fun and help her miss Fleur less—at least for a little while. "Okay." She sighed. "Thanks, Dad."

She went into the house, put on her boots, and came back out holding her riding hat by the chin strap.

"All set!" Mr. Danes started the engine.

It was only a few minutes' drive to
Marshall's Stables. Mr. Danes and Steph
went toward the office just as Judy Marshall
was coming out. She was a slim woman
with dark hair, a round face, and friendly
blue eyes.

"Hi! You must be Steph. Nice to meet
you," she said, smiling.

"Nice to meet you, too, Mrs. Marshall,"

Steph said, making an effort to be polite. She still wasn't sure that she wanted to do this.

"Call me Judy. Everyone does. Come and meet the ponies." She turned to Mr. Danes. "Steph will be fine now. We'll look after her."

"See you later then, sweetie. Have a good time."

"Bye, Dad." Steph watched him walk away and then followed Judy toward the main stable block.

The smart redbrick buildings were around two sides of a square. Two smallish ponies were tied up outside the tack room. A boy and a girl in riding gear stood waiting to mount.

"Judy? Someone's on the phone for you!" a voice called.

"Coming!" Judy answered. She turned to Steph. "Sorry, but I need to take this call. Why don't you have a look around? Just check with a staff member before you take a pony out, okay?"

Steph nodded, smiling awkwardly. "Thanks, Judy."

She walked toward the loose boxes. The ponies turned to look at her, twitching their ears curiously. Steph went along the row, stroking and patting each one in turn. Their names were on the doors: Jiggy, Binky, Misty, Lady, and Rags. They were all nice, but none of them were Fleur. She fondly remembered the little chestnut pony's silky mane.

At the end of the row, there was an empty box. As Steph reached it there was a bright flash and sparkling rainbow mist filled the walls of the box. Rainbow drops settled on her skin, glittering in the afternoon light.

"Oh!" Steph blinked, trying to see through the strange mist.

As it slowly cleared, she saw that there was in fact a pony in there after all. It was a handsome black-and-white piebald with a broad white stripe down its nose and large deep-violet eyes. How could she

have missed it before? But Steph couldn't deny he was there now and as the pony looked at her inquisitively, Steph felt her heart melt just a little.

"Hello, you!" she crooned gently. She'd never seen a pony with eyes that color. Maybe she could ride him. *But just so I can tell Dad that I did*, Steph thought quickly.

Opening the door, she went inside and lifted her hand to stroke the pony's satiny cheek. It turned to look at her.

"Can you help me, please?" it asked in a velvety neigh.

About the
AUTHOR

Sue Bentley's books for children often include animals, fairies, and wildlife. She lives in Northampton, England, and enjoys reading, going to the movies, and watching the birds on the feeders outside her window. She loves horses, which she thinks are all completely magical. One of her favorite books is *Black Beauty*, which she must have read at least ten times. At school she was always getting scolded for daydreaming, but she now knows that she was storing up ideas for when she became a writer. Sue has met and owned many animals, but the wild creatures in her life hold a special place in her heart.

Don't miss these
Magic Ponies books!

Don't miss these
Magic Kitten books!

Don't miss these
Magic Puppy books!